A WOODLAND MYSTERY ®

The Mystery of the Dark Old House

A WOODLAND MYSTERY
By Irene Schultz

Hogan Cedars Elementary School
1770 S.E. Fleming Avenue
Gresham, OR 97080

Wright Group
McGraw-Hill

To my husband, Jerome Schultz, who helped me with his faithful love and support

The Mystery of the Dark Old House
Text copyright © Irene Schultz
Illustrations copyright © Wright Group/McGraw-Hill
Cover and illustrations by Taylor Bruce
Map illustration by Alicia Kramer

Woodland Mysteries® is a registered trademark of Wright Group/McGraw-Hill.

Published by Wright Group/McGraw-Hill, a division of the McGraw-Hill Companies, Inc. All rights reserved. No part of this publication may be reproduced or distributed in any form or by any means, or stored in a database or retrieval system, without the prior written consent of Wright Group/McGraw-Hill, including, but not limited to, network or other electronic storage or transmission, or broadcast for distance learning.

Wright Group/McGraw-Hill
19201 120th Avenue NE, Suite 100
Bothell, WA 98011
www.WrightGroup.com

Printed in the United States of America

10 9 8 7

ISBN: 0-7802-7242-0
ISBN: 0-7802-7940-9 (6-pack)

What family solves mysteries...has adventures all over the world...and loves oatmeal cookies?

It's the Woodlanders!

Sammy Westburg (10 years old)
His sister Kathy Westburg (13)
His brother Bill Westburg (14)
His best friend Dave Briggs (16)
His best grown-up friend Mrs. Tandy
And Mop, their little dog!

The children all lost their parents, but with Mrs. Tandy have made their own family.

Why are they called the Woodlanders? Because they live in a big house in the Bluff Lake woods. On Woodland Street!

Together they find fun, mystery, and adventure. What are they up to now?

Read on!

Meet the Woodlanders!

Sammy Westburg
Sammy is a ten-year-old wonder! He's big for his fifth-grade class, and big-mouthed, too. He has wild hair and makes awful spider faces. Even so, you can't help liking him.

Bill Westburg
Bill, fourteen, is friendly and strong, and only one inch taller than his brother Sammy. He loves Sammy, but pokes him to make him be quiet! He's in junior high.

Kathy Westburg
Kathy, thirteen, is small, shy, and smart. She wants to be a doctor someday! She loves to be with Dave, and her brothers kid her about it. She's in junior high, too.

Dave Briggs

Dave, sixteen, is tall and blond. He can't walk, so he uses a wheelchair and drives a special car. He likes coaching high-school sports, solving mysteries, and reading. And Kathy!

Mrs. Tandy

Sometimes the kids call her Mrs. T. She's Becky Tandy, their tall, thin, caring friend. She's always ready for a new adventure, and for making cookies!

Mop

Mop is the family's little tan dog. Sometimes they have to leave him behind with friends. But he'd much rather be running after Sammy.

Table of Contents

Chapter 1:
The Old Bell House

Every kid in Bluff Lake knew about the old
Bell House.

Most said it was haunted.

Mr. and Mrs. Bell used to live there,

but they had died years ago. Then the dark old house was closed up.

It stood like a lonely giant on the cliff near the lake.

Kids used to play in the yard there. But one night two of them saw a light in a window. They got scared and ran home.

The grown-ups said it must have been the setting sun, not a light from inside the house. But after that, most children stayed away. ✶

One fall day, the Woodland family decided to walk to the old Bell House to pick some wild plums.

On the way there, Bill Westburg, fourteen, teased his ten-year-old brother Sammy. He said, "Aren't you afraid of the old house?

"Somebody saw something move in

the grass there last year. They say it was a ghost!"

Sammy said, "I'm not scared. Some other guys said they saw an elf there this summer. But YOU said there were no such things as ghosts and elves."

He stuck out his chest and marched along like a soldier.

Sammy's thirteen-year-old sister Kathy smiled at him. She said, "Well, even ghosts would be afraid of you, Sammy!"

Mrs. Tandy said, "I wouldn't care if there WERE elves. That house has the best wild plums in Bluff Lake. I pick them every year!"

Soon they came to the old Bell House.

Sixteen-year-old Dave Briggs rolled up the driveway in his wheelchair.

He said, "I heard somebody broke some windows here this spring. I guess that's why they're all boarded up."

Sammy said, "Yeah. That was REAL smart. The police found out who they were and they had to pay a fine."

Mrs. Tandy said, "Albert and Ann Strong had those boards put up. They used to be the Bells' best friends, you know."

They saw a squirrel running around in the dry leaves.

Bill said, "Look at those bright yellow leaves. They must be from those big maple trees."

4

Sammy said, "It's so nice here, I can't see why people are so afraid of it."

Bill said, "Maybe they're scared some weird kid like you will come racing down this drive way and bump into them."

Sammy said, "Very funny. How would you like a prize for being so funny?"

He dropped a handful of leaves onto Bill's head and ran off.

Dave wheeled along in front of the others. He was almost to the house.

He called, "Hey, look at this! A chipmunk just ran up to my chair and sat on its hind legs, like a pet. It's so tame!"

Kathy said, "Oh, I love it here!" She spun like a top in the sunshine.

Sammy ran from the driveway to a path that led to the left.

Kathy followed him.

Bill came next, pushing Dave's chair.

Mrs. Tandy was right behind them.

They stopped at the side of the house to look around.

All of a sudden Kathy grabbed Sammy's arm. She pointed to a huge tree, way over near the cliff.

Everyone looked.

They all stood as still as stones, but their hearts were jumping.

In front of the tree stood a small man, about a foot shorter than Sammy.

He gave them a wild look. Then he jumped behind the tree.

They were so scared, no one could move an inch.

At last Bill made himself walk a few steps to the left. From there he could see behind the tree.

But no one was there.

The little man had disappeared.

Chapter 2:
Was It an Elf?

Bill said, "He's gone!"

Sammy looked all around. He said, "He can't just be GONE! Did he fall off the cliff?"

Bill sneaked to the edge of the cliff. He said, "He's not down there. He's just gone."

Sammy said, "I know you're going to laugh at me, but do you know what that was? It was an ELF. Just like those kids said."

Bill laughed. "Oh, come off it, Sammy."

But even in the warm sunshine, he suddenly felt cold. He said, "You know elves aren't REAL."

Sammy made his worst face ... his poison-spider face ... at Bill. He said, "Yeah? Then how do you explain what we BOTH just saw?

"He had a man's head. And a man's body. And short legs. He was an elf."

Kathy had felt a little scared ... until she heard that.

She said, "Wait a minute, Sammy.

Someone was there, all right.

"But it was probably just someone trying to scare us. Not an elf."

Mrs. Tandy said, "That's right, Sammy ... a child, maybe."

Dave wheeled himself to the edge of the cliff and looked over.

He called, "Well, Bill is right. Whoever it was is gone now. And Kathy's right. Whoever it was is just trying to scare us."

Mrs. Tandy said, "I really hate to give up on my plum jelly ... just because someone's trying to keep us away."

11

Sammy said, "Me, too. Do you think we should still get the plums, Dave?"

Just then a cloud covered the sun.

The wind began to blow.

A board on the house began to knock against the wall.

The leaves on the trees started to move in the wind. They made a whispering sound.

The sky turned dark and mean.

The warm fall afternoon turned cold and gray.

Suddenly Sammy headed back down the path ... back the way they had come ... back to the driveway.

Kathy and Mrs. Tandy followed him, fast.

Bill pushed Dave along at a half-run.

The wheelchair rattled as they dashed along the driveway.

They were almost flying out to the

street, they were so scared.

And they all kept on running.

Only when they came to their own driveway did they slow down. They were worn-out.

Mrs. Tandy panted, "Our house sure looks good to me!"

Sammy said, "Me, too. I'm never going back to the old Bell House again. It WAS an elf, you know!"

Dave said, "I'd like to know who it really was, but I don't want to go back to find out."

Kathy said, "I don't want to talk about it, I'm so scared. And I don't even believe in elves!"

Mrs. Tandy said, "I sure will miss that plum jelly.

"But wild horses can't drag me back there with that crazy elf thing around. Oh my, I'm tired from running."

The Woodlanders dragged themselves up to the front porch.

They could hear their shaggy dog Mop barking from inside the house.

They opened the door just in time to hear the phone ring.

Mop raced in circles.

Dave wheeled to the phone. He picked it up in the dining room.

Sammy yelled, "I'll get it!" and ran into the bedroom.

So both Sammy and Dave heard a slow, ghostly voice say, "This is a warning. Stay away from the old Bell House."

Then the phone clicked. And the ghost caller was gone.

Chapter 3:
A Hunt for Plums and Answers

Sammy came running into the dining room.

He yelled, "Hey, do you know who that was? It sounded just like a man trying to sound like a ghost! But do you know who it REALLY was?"

"Who?" everyone asked at the same time.

Sammy said, "It was the elf! That's who it was, because he told us to stay away from the old Bell House. Hey, I never knew an elf could use a telephone!"

Dave said, "This elf guy is making me mad. First he appears, then he disappears.

"And now he tries to scare us again, on our own phone! I wonder how he got our phone number, anyway?"

Bill said, "I'd like to go back and find out how he pulled that hiding trick."

Sammy made a fist. He said, "Me, too. And that little man better not try any funny stuff with me again."

Kathy said, "I guess I'd go back. Just

so I don't have to wonder who he is anymore."

Mrs. Tandy said, "It's easier to be brave in our own house, so right now I think I'd like to take another look, too."

Dave said, "We all want to go back. So let's do it tomorrow, when it's light out."

Sunday morning, the Woodlanders sat around the kitchen table.

Bill was chewing on a muffin. He said, "OK, let's plan our trip back to the old Bell House."

Sammy said, "I've got a plan already. But first give me the muffins before the muffin pig gets them all."

Bill said, "Look who's calling ME a muffin pig. That's your fourth one."

Sammy stuck out his tongue.

He said, "Well, I'm only ten and a growing boy. And anyway, I'm going to need a lot of energy."

Dave asked, "What's your plan, Sammy?"

Sammy said, "This time we can take Mop with us, right over to where we saw the little elf man.

"He will sniff him out. Then I'll grab the elf man and sit on him.

"On second thought, I'd better not. He'd be mashed flat, and we'd all end up in jail."

Dave laughed. "I think we just have to go without a plan and see what happens."

Mrs. Tandy said, "Well, I have one plan you'll like, I think. Let's make sandwiches for lunch, and have a picnic!"

Sammy said, "Perfect! First the snack, then ATTACK!"

Kathy said, "Let's put the sandwiches into paper bags. Then we can use the bags for picking plums later."

Mrs. Tandy said, "Here's cold turkey, and home-baked ham, and lettuce, and bread."

Kathy added, "Here are apples and cheese."

Bill said, "And we can take pop and cupcakes."

So they packed five bags, one for each of them.

Dave said, "Here, give me the pop cans. I'll take the lunch bags on my lap, too."

At last they were heading up the

driveway of the old Bell House. The sun was shining bright and warm.

Mop raced after a squirrel or two.

Birds were singing.

Kathy said, "What was I so afraid of before?"

Bill had the same thought. He said, "I know what you mean. Why did we ever run, guys? I feel sort of stupid now."

They walked up the path and over to the big tree. They put down the five lunch bags and the pop cans.

Sammy said, "Let's take a good look

around here. This is right where the little man was standing. I bet I can figure out where he went."

Kathy said, "Here's where he was. Right by this big sawed-off trunk, next to the main tree."

Sammy said, "I'm going down the side of the cliff in back of the tree. Maybe there's a cave down there ... and he hid in it."

Bill said, "Then I'm going with you."

The two boys looked over the edge of the cliff.

They saw a few paths leading down, and started down slowly.

Bill said, "Watch out for poison ivy, Sammy!"

They went down to the bottom of the cliff, looking for a cave ... then up on another path ... then down again ... then up again.

23

Sammy said, "There isn't any cave. The ground must have opened up and swallowed that guy!"

Kathy, Dave, and Mrs. Tandy had looked over every inch of the deep grass within twenty feet of the tree. Then they had searched all around the huge yard.

But by noon they still had no idea where the little man had gone.

They all met near the tree.

Sammy said, "Who cares about him, anyway? Let's eat lunch!"

Mrs. Tandy gasped, "My goodness, look at that!"

She was pointing to the pile of lunch bags. She said, "We must have dropped a lunch somewhere. There are only four bags here."

Mop ran over and sniffed the bags.

Sammy said, "No way, Mrs. T.! I counted them when we put them down.

I KNOW we put five of them there."

Kathy said, "Maybe Mop took one."

Sammy asked, "But wouldn't there be some scraps of brown paper around if Mop got one?"

Kathy said, "Maybe not. Maybe he took it away to eat it."

Dave said, "Well, I know it wasn't Mop who took it."

Bill said, "How do you know?"

Dave said, "Because one of the pop cans is gone, too. No dog I know would take a can of pop and run off with it."

They all stared at each other.

Finally, Mrs. Tandy said what they had all been thinking. "Well, it looks like that sneaky elf guy stole himself some lunch."

Chapter 4:
Mop Finds a Princess

Kathy said, "Lucky we packed so much food. Even with only four bags, we still have lots to eat. It's just a little scary, that's all."

Sammy said, "I wonder how he did it? But let's eat, before he steals the rest!"

They spread out a blanket and had their picnic under the tree.

Bill asked, "What do you think we should do next?"

Dave said, "We've looked over every inch around the tree. I don't know if we should even look for the little food-grabber anymore."

Sammy said, "Well, if you ask me, I say we keep looking for him.

"I'm going to squeeze that chocolate cupcake he stole right out of him!"

Kathy said, "Come on, Sammy. Why ruin our whole day looking for him? Let's just pick plums."

Sammy said, "OK, then we can go home and make the jelly. I'm going to be Mrs. T.'s number-one taster!"

Bill laughed. "Then, good-bye, jelly!"

Kathy said, "Hey, what's wrong with Mop?"

Mop had been running around begging for scraps of food. All of a sudden he stood still.

He lifted his head in the air and sniffed. His ears went back. He stopped wagging his tail. He growled.

Bill said, "He must smell another dog!"

Suddenly Mop ran off barking into the tall grass.

Then all of a sudden they heard two dogs barking!

Sammy said, "Hey! Sounds like Mop found a friend to play with!"

They saw the tall grass move.

At last, Mop ran out toward them.

Another dog ran after him.

The two dogs began biting at each other in play. They rolled over on each other.

They yipped. They ran away from each other. They bumped. They jumped and fell on each other.

Sammy said, "That's just how Bill and I played when we were little!"

The new dog wasn't as tall as Mop, but it was much longer.

Sammy said, "That's one of those hot-dog dogs, a big one."

Kathy said, "I think it's a girl. She's beautiful. Smooth and black, like a seal."

Mrs. Tandy said, "Where did she come from, I wonder?"

Dave said, "Let's get her over here,

guys. Maybe she has a tag that says who owns her."

Bill called, "Here, boy! Here, Mop!"

Mop came bouncing over. His new friend ran over with him.

Sammy caught the new dog by the collar. He said, "Nice dog. I hope she knows she's a nice dog, and won't bite me!"

Kathy asked, "What do the tags say?"

Sammy said, "Let's see. This one is her license number. And this one is a rabies tag. Oh, here's the owner's name."

Mrs. Tandy said, "Well?"

Sammy said, "Wow! You're not going to believe this! This dog belongs to the Strongs!"

Bill said, "How weird! What's she doing way over here then? The Strongs live in the middle of town, about ten blocks from here."

Kathy said, "So this dog's about a mile from home. Do you think she could find her way back by herself?"

Mrs. Tandy said, "What's her name, Sammy? Does it say?"

Sammy said, "The tag says PRINCESS on it. Maybe we'd better take Princess back to the Strongs."

Dave said, "Yep, we should. If you put Mop's leash on Princess's collar, I'll hold her until we go."

Mrs. Tandy said, "It's a pretty long walk to the Strongs and home."

Dave said, "Maybe we should walk to our house with the pup, and then I'll drive us over to the Strongs' house from there."

Sammy said, "OK, but first we have to get those plums!"

They all got to work picking plums ... except Sammy.

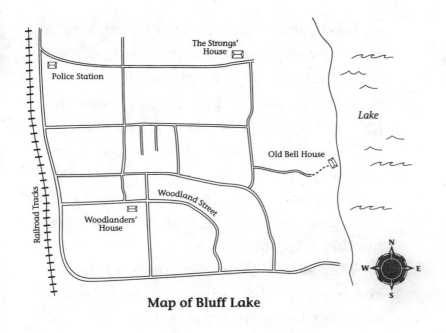

Map of Bluff Lake

He chased Bill with a soft, rotten plum.

He threw it and missed.

Mop went bouncing after it.

He gave it a sniff. Then he ate it!

Bill said, "Yuck, Sammy! Look what you made Mop do!"

33

Mrs. Tandy said, "It won't hurt him a bit. Anyway, let's head home now. We have four full bags of plums!"

Sammy said, "Dave, give me the leash. I'll walk Princess, the hot dog."

They all started back down the driveway.

Kathy said, "It's getting dark again all of a sudden ... maybe there's going to be another bad storm."

They could hear thousands of leaves moving in the wind. Then entire branches began to wave wildly.

Mrs. Tandy said, "It's only one thirty, but it's almost as dark as night. And the house is looking scary again!"

They all turned to look at it from the driveway.

Bill said, "It reminds me of the ghost movie we saw last week on TV. Remember that dark old house, and the roar of thunder, just like now?"

Sammy said, "Holy cats! Do you see what I see?"

Dave gasped. "Wow! Is that a light in the little window? Right there! Under the point of the roof!"

Just as he said that, the light went out.

Kathy said slowly, "Someone IS in the old Bell House."

The Woodlanders stood still, there in the dark. A flash of lightning and a roar of thunder broke their stares.

Once again, they were as scared as rabbits.

They ran wildly with Dave's chair, while Bill screamed for Mop.

They ran all the way home, dragging the new dog with them.

Chapter 5:
The Mystery Dog

As the Woodlanders ran up to their house, the phone rang.

Sammy moaned, "Oh, no, not another call.

"Is it the elf man AGAIN?"

Kathy got the door open, and ran to the phone.

"Hello?"

She heard an angry man's voice. "Dog robbers! Dog robbers! Return that dog! You are bad children! And that awful bad woman. You should all be ashamed!"

Then Kathy heard choking sounds. The phone clicked dead.

"Was it him?" everyone asked.

She told them what the man had said.

Mrs. Tandy said, "Well, he must have been watching us the whole time.

"He must think we stole the dog.

"We'd better call the Strongs right away and tell them about finding Princess there."

Kathy said, "You know, I think the man was crying when he hung up."

38

Sammy said, "I bet he's crying because he's going to be put in jail for breaking into the old Bell House. And maybe for stealing Princess, too."

Bill said, "What I wonder is, where does he call from?"

Sammy said, "Maybe there's still a phone in the old Bell House."

Bill said, "No, there couldn't be. No one's lived there for years."

Dave said, "Well, let's at least call the Strongs and get their dog back to them."

When he called, a grandmotherly voice said, "Hello?"

Dave said, "Hello, Mrs. Strong. This is Dave Briggs. We found your dog Princess about a mile from your house."

Dave heard Mrs. Strong gasp.

He went on. "Don't worry. We have her here. We can bring her over right away if you want."

Mrs. Strong said, "Oh my goodness!"

Dave said, "She's OK. Really. We will be right there."

Mrs. Strong said, "Oh, no. Wait a minute, dear. Let me think. Stay on the phone."

Dave held his hand over the phone and whispered, "It's weird. She sounds like she doesn't want the dog."

At last she said, "Hello, Dave? The dog you found? She belongs to us, but she lives with someone else.

"Will you do my husband and me a big favor? Do you know where the old Bell House is?

"Take the dog up the driveway there and let her out. She can find her way home from there."

Dave said, "Are you sure that's what you want?"

She said, "Yes, Dave. And thank you!"

Dave said, "If you say so! Good-bye!"

He told the others what she had said.

Sammy said, "Wow. Something funny's going on here! Who ever heard of a dog that lives a mile away from its owners?"

Bill said, "And who ever heard of dropping off a dog in front of an empty house?"

41

Kathy said, "And why didn't she tell us where Princess really lives? We'd have left her there."

Sammy said, "Hey, do you know what I think? I think Mrs. Strong has gone goofy."

Dave shook his head. "Mrs. Strong didn't sound goofy at all to me. She sounded just like she always does."

Kathy said, "Do you know what I think? I think Princess lives at the old Bell House!"

Mrs. Tandy said, "Alone?"

Bill said, "No, I know who lives there with her!"

Sammy shouted, "I know, too! The little man, or kid, or elf, or whatever he is!

"He lives in the old Bell House!

"He broke in, and he lives there!

"He's a crook! And Mrs. Strong is his partner in crime!"

Sammy made his hands into fists. He began to wave them in the air.

He said, "I'm going to break in and catch him. I'm going to stop that little thief once and for all.

"And wait until Dr. Strong finds out about his wife!"

Kathy said, "Just a minute, Sammy. If YOU go into the house, YOU'LL be breaking the law.

"Anyway, I don't think the little man is really a crook."

Mrs. Tandy said, "Maybe he just needed a place to live."

Kathy said, "The question is ... how does Mrs. Strong know him ... and why does she let him keep her dog?"

Bill said, "Who knows. But SOME-THING is going on in that house. And I vote we go there and find out what it is."

Dave said, "Well, I'll drive. Put on your raincoats, everybody. And get your flashlights.

"And get Princess, Sammy."

As they piled into the car, the thunder roared again.

Sammy shouted, "Even thunder can't stop us now! Make way for the Woodlanders!"

And off they drove to the old Bell House.

Chapter 6:
A Dark Discovery

Dave drove up the driveway of the old house and stopped.

They all sat in the car, looking at the house in the rain.

Bill said, "This place gives me the

creeps. It's hard to believe anyone would want to live here."

Kathy said, "It's hard to believe we ever saw a light in that little window."

Sammy jumped out of the car. He ran up the wide steps to the front porch. He pounded on the front door.

BANG! BANG! BANG!

Bill called, "Hey, what are you doing, Sammy?" He jumped out of the car, and ran up the steps, too.

Sammy said, "What else? I'm trying to get the little man to open the door."

Dave called, "Let him pound, Bill. I can't think of any better way to try to get the man's attention."

So Sammy pounded some more. Then, both boys pounded on every boarded-up window.

Bill said, "Looks like nobody's going to answer."

Sammy said, "I'll find him. I don't care if I drown in the rain.

"I'm going to talk to him.

"I bet I could pull off one of those boards. I could sneak in and find him."

Bill said, "Oh, no, you won't."

Sammy stuck out his tongue. He said, "You just want to keep me from being the one who finds him."

Bill said, "I don't want to keep you from being a hero, I want to keep you from being thrown in jail."

At last they went back to the car.

Mrs. Tandy rolled down the back window to talk to them.

All of a sudden, Princess jumped off of her lap ... and out the car window!

Bill shouted, "There she goes, onto the porch!"

From the front seat Kathy shouted, "Look, she's coming down the steps again.

47

She's headed for the cliff!"

Kathy jumped out of the car and ran with Bill and Sammy to catch Princess.

Then she stopped and turned toward the car.

Dave shouted, "Go on, Kathy! I can handle the wheelchair myself!"

He banged it out of the car from behind his seat, opened it wide, and swung himself into it.

Sammy was way out in front. The rain was coming down hard.

His shoes slip-slopped with each step. But he didn't care. He stayed close to Princess.

The dog ran up to the huge old tree and stopped. She stood for a minute beside the big sawed-off trunk next to it.

Sammy saw his chance to grab her. He made a dive.

He got his arms around her. He fell

against the stump.

Suddenly he was falling, bottom first. With Princess in his arms, he fell about four feet!

He landed on a floor as hard as stone. Everything was dark and closed in, like a cave.

He shouted, "Help! Bill! Help!"

By then Bill had reached the tree stump. In the blinding rain, he couldn't see where Sammy went.

He ran around the giant tree and the stump. He called, "Sammy, where are you?"

Kathy ran up to Bill. They both heard Sammy call from below.

Kathy said, "Oh, no! Has he fallen off the cliff?"

They looked over the edge, but didn't see him.

Bill shouted, "Where are you, Sammy?"

Sammy yelled, "Help me, Bill! I'm in here!"

Mrs. Tandy ran up.

She said, "My lands! That tree stump is yelling!"

Dave wheeled up to them just in time to hear her. He said, "Sammy's inside the stump?"

Bill shouted, "How did you get in there?"

Sammy yelled, "All I know is I fell against that sawed-off trunk ... and landed down here!"

In an instant, Kathy, Bill, and Mrs.

Tandy were on their knees in the wet grass.

They pushed against the side of the tree stump. It swung in easily.

And there was Sammy, down below.

Princess was nowhere in sight.

Sammy climbed back up out of the stump.

Bill grabbed him and hugged him.

So did Kathy and Mrs. Tandy!

Bill said, "I can't believe you fell INTO a tree. Everyone else has brothers who fall OUT of trees."

Then Kathy lay on her stomach, and shined her flashlight inside the tree trunk.

Sammy said, "It's a cave in there, Kathy. That's how the little man hides until people go away. Then out he pops, free as a bird."

Dave leaned over to look inside. He said, "If it's a cave, it's not a real one. It's made of cement."

Sammy said, "Oh, come on. How can you tell it's cement? Who are you, Sherlock Holmes?"

Dave said, "I KNOW it's cement. Look there."

Kathy kept shining her light down to the cave floor.

They all crowded around and looked into the opening.

Across the floor some words were written in crooked print. It looked like a child's finger had written in wet cement. It said, "Gordon Bell lives here."

Kathy said, "Sammy, do you know what this is?"

Sammy looked proud. He said, "Sure! I found the hole where the little man hides."

Mrs. Tandy said, "My word, Sammy! You've found more than that!"

Bill whispered, "It looks like you've found a tunnel, Sammy!

"And I bet it leads straight into the old Bell House!"

Chapter 7:
The Underground Tunnel

The Woodlanders looked at each other.

Then they heard Princess yip in the tunnel. She sounded very far away.

Sammy said, "Hey, I forgot about Princess! I'm going after her!"

Then he jumped back into the tree stump. He started running down the tunnel.

Bill called, "Stop, Sammy! Stop! Wait for the rest of us!"

They heard a noise like a door banging shut, far away.

Mrs. Tandy got down on her hands and knees.

She yelled into the tree trunk, "Sammy! Come back!"

Kathy was really scared. She said, "Dave, what should we do?"

Dave asked, "Did he have his flashlight with him?"

Kathy cried, "Yes!"

Dave said, "That's good. Come on. Help me in. I know it's against the law, but we have to go after him."

Dave lowered himself from his wheelchair to the wet grass.

Bill folded the chair and put it down into the tunnel.

He jumped in after it. He un-folded it, and held the tree-stump door open for Dave.

Dave lowered himself from the ground above into his chair.

Kathy helped Mrs. Tandy down next.

Dave said, "Come on, guys! Quick!"

They all turned on their flashlights and raced along the tunnel.

The rest of the tunnel was about six feet high, and six feet wide.

Bill called softly, "Sammy? Where are you?"

No one answered.

The tunnel ended at a wooden door.

Bill said, "Holy cats! I bet Sammy's on the other side of that door."

Mrs. Tandy said, "Where do you suppose that goes?"

Dave said, "Probably to the basement of the old house."

Bill called again softly, "Sammy! Sammy!"

They heard a knock from the other side of the door.

A scared voice said, "Hey, who's out there? Is that you, guys?"

Bill called, "Sammy! Come back out here!"

Sammy said, "I can't. I can't open the door.

"There's no handle on this side, and I

can't push it open ... and Bill ... I'm scared in here."

Bill said, "Stand back, Sammy!" He ran up to the door and pushed it. It swung wide open, away from him, into a dark room.

They shined their flashlights through the open doorway.

There stood Sammy.

His face looked red.

He said, "I'm SO glad you're here. I was scared.

"And I can't find Princess!

"And I don't know where we are! And I dropped my flashlight. And now it doesn't work. And it's dark."

He ended with, "Gosh, Bill."

He ran up to his brother and threw his arms around him.

Bill said, "Sammy, don't you ever THINK before you jump into trouble?"

Dave said, "Are you OK, Sammy?"

Sammy said, "I'm OK now that you're all here. But where are we?"

Dave said, "I think in the basement of the old Bell House. Here, let's prop open this door so we can get out again."

Kathy propped it open with a loose board she found.

Mrs. Tandy asked, "What do we do now? What about Princess?"

Kathy said, "Well, we can't just leave Princess here alone. If that little man isn't around, she will starve!"

They shined their lights on another door in front of them.

Bill said, "That must lead to the rest of the basement. Let's go, guys."

He pushed on the door, and it swung open easily.

He said, "Hey! Princess could easily have come through this door by herself!"

Dave said, "I see how these doors work. See, there's a rope to pull. It's down near the floor.

"No wonder we couldn't find it back in the other room. We were looking for a door knob higher up."

They tip-toed into a large room.

They shined their lights all around.

It was a workshop.

There were hammers, screwdrivers, and other tools. They were hanging on the wall in neat rows.

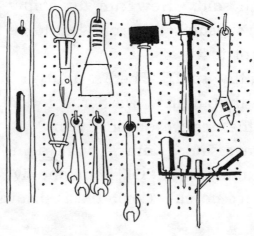

In front of a worktable was a long bench.

Kathy said, "That bench would be too low to sit on, and too high for me to stand on."

Sammy said, "But it would be just right for a little elf man to stand on."

Mrs. Tandy said, "Do you see how clean everything is?   Not a spiderweb anywhere."

They aimed their lights higher.   Even the ceiling beams were clean.

Bill said, "How can an empty house be this clean?   Some one has to be taking care of it."

Kathy said, "There's a dryer and ... isn't that a new washer?   It looks just like the one we got last year!"

Dave said, "Kathy, you're right."

Sammy said, "OK, some one lives here. And it's no elf!   Come on!   Upstairs!   I'm not scared anymore."

Just then they heard the rattle of chains ... coming from upstairs.

Chapter 8:
Get Out!

Sammy whispered, "Yikes. NOW I'm scared. What was that?"

Dave whispered, "Shh... just keep listening."

They all froze, but they didn't hear another sound.

Sammy asked, "Do you think we should get out of here? Do you think Mrs. Tandy should go get Chief Hemster?

"Those sounded like ghost chains. It sounded like the haunted house on Halloween.

"Or maybe those were BONES hitting the floor."

Bill said, "Give me a break! I'm going up to the first floor. I'll sneak up the steps first to take a look."

Dave said, "OK, but come right back down for us."

Bill shined his flashlight on the steps. He went up softly, like a cat sneaking up on a bird.

He opened the door at the top. The room was dark. The boards on the windows kept the sunlight out.

He shined his light around. All he saw was a big entrance hall with a bench in it.

No one was there.

Bill sneaked back down the steps. He said, "No one's around. Boy, it feels weird hunting through someone else's house!"

They lifted Dave in his chair to the first floor.

With their flashlights on, they sneaked slowly across the dark hall.

They saw a doorway, then another large room.

"Holy cow!"

"Yikes!"

It was full of big white shapes!

Sammy said, "Aw, it's just a bunch of furniture with white sheets on it.

"See, that must be a couch. And there's a table. And some chairs.

Big deal ... it's a living room."

Bill said, "Well, Princess isn't in here. Let's keep going."

Kathy called, "Here's a dining room and a kitchen. There's furniture and an old stove and stuff.

"But you know what? It's all dusty. I guess no one uses these rooms."

Dave said, "Let's go upstairs, OK?"

Bill and Sammy pulled his chair to the second floor.

Dave said, "Thanks, you guys."

Sammy bragged, "No problem. It was easy."

Still, he stopped to rest for a minute.

While they stood there, Bill said, "Hey, listen! It sounds like Princess is running down some stairs! In a room over there!"

They all heard a faint bark.

They heard toenails scratching down wooden steps.

Then the sound was gone.

Bill whispered, "There's got to be another stairway in this house."

Sammy whispered, "Wait a minute!"

He ran along the hall and went into the room where they thought they heard Princess.

But he came right back.

He said, "There's nothing back there but a table and a bed, all covered with sheets. And a closet that's totally empty."

Dave said, "Well, let's keep searching."

He pushed open the door nearest to them, at the top of the steps.

This room was big, and lined with book shelves. The windows weren't boarded up, so light poured in.

Kathy said, "Wow! It's a library!"

There was a small red leather arm-chair, child-sized ...

a fine desk with a chair

a couch

hundreds of books

... and a set of wooden steps on wheels, for getting books off the top shelves.

Sammy ran over and climbed the library steps.

He put a leg on each side, as if he were riding a horse.

Bill grinned and said, "Sammy the cowboy rides again!"

Mrs. Tandy said, "What a great room! All these wonderful books!"

Bill said, "I could spend a year here."

Sammy said, "Why don't you? I'll come and get you next September."

Dave said, "Come on, let's look at the rest of the place.

"This isn't where we saw that light.

71

This is the back of the house, and one floor too low."

Kathy said, "There's got to be a third floor here. That's where the mystery man's bedroom must be. But how do we get up to it?"

Bill had an idea. He said, "Let's check out the room Sammy looked into again. Really carefully this time."

Sammy said, "Don't you trust me?"

Dave said, "You were in a hurry, Sammy. And we HAVE to find the way to that upper floor.

"So let's go take one more look. That is where the sound came from."

They went down the hall and into that bedroom.

Sammy pointed suddenly to the old bed against one wall.

There was something on the bed.

He whispered, "That wasn't here when

I checked before."

Across the bed lay a sheet of paper about as big as a pillowcase.

It said GET OUT in letters a foot tall.

A skull and crossbones were drawn on it.

Chapter 9:
The Secret Door

Bill walked over to the bed.

He picked up the big sheet of paper.

He said, "Wow! Here's the final proof. Now we KNOW he's here."

Kathy said, "I've been thinking ... what if the little man is hiding because he's afraid of US?"

Mrs. Tandy said, "He IS trying awfully hard to stay hidden. What a sad way to spend your life!"

Dave said, "Well, we have to find him, whether he wants us to or not. For Princess's sake.

"So let's find out how he got into this room to leave this warning ... and then out so fast.

"Somewhere there has to be a hidden door. Maybe we can find a secret button or a hollow wall."

Dave, Kathy, and Mrs. Tandy began to press and tap on every part of the old wallpaper. They didn't find a thing.

Sammy and Bill checked the closet.

Bill said, "We've gone over every inch of this room. Zero!"

Kathy said, "Well, back to square one."

Mrs. Tandy sat on the edge of the bed.

She said, "I'm puzzled. The walls don't have a hidden door, and the floor doesn't either. The closet is solid.

"That can't leave anything much to be a secret door, or even a secret-door switch."

Kathy said, "All that's left is the ceiling. And there's no panel there. All it's got is the light fixture."

Sammy said, "So let's check that!"

Bill was looking at the bed. He said, "Will somebody tell me why the sheet is all dirty at the head of the bed?"

At that moment they heard a sound coming from the hall.

Sammy whispered, "It's those chains again."

They all went into the hallway.

Sammy pointed up in the air.

He said, "What's that?"

They all looked up.

Above them, in the dim light of the hall, they saw a large square cut into the ceiling wallpaper.

Dave said, "That's it! That's got to be a trap door to the third floor!"

In a second, Sammy dashed into the library. He called, "Come on, Bill!"

Bill said, "I'm right with you! Those library steps will be perfect!"

They rolled the steps into the hall and underneath the trap door.

But before anyone could get a good hold on them, Sammy ran up the steps.

He gave a hard push on the trap door ... a very hard push.

The trap door didn't move, but the steps did.

They rolled right out from under him.

Sammy fell to the floor.

He lay very still.

Blood ran out of a cut on his head and onto the rug.

Kathy gave a little scream and dropped down on her knees next to her brother.

She said, "Sammy, say something! Wake up!"

She held her hand hard against the cut. She said, "We have to stop the bleeding."

Dave said, "We don't have anything clean to bandage it with. And we need water. We have to get help, Mrs. Tandy."

All of a sudden they heard the noise of chains again, from the panel above them. Now they saw what made the noise.

One end of the panel lowered on chains.

The panel WAS a trap door!

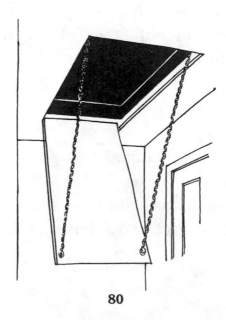

They couldn't see into it, but they heard the voice of the little man.

He said, "Here! I'm throwing down some clean dish towels. And some bandages. In a minute I'll lower a pail of water."

A heap of towels and bandages landed at their feet ... then a pail came down on a rope.

The Woodlanders were so surprised, they couldn't speak at first.

Then Bill finally said, "Thanks, thanks so much!"

With a long dish towel, Kathy tied a bandage pad against Sammy's head.

Then she dipped another towel into the pail. She patted cold water all over Sammy's face.

Mrs. Tandy started down the hall. She said, "I'll get a doctor. My poor Sammy!"

Chapter 10:
The Voice from the Attic

A sleepy voice from the floor said, "Why are you getting a doctor? Is someone hurt?"

It was Sammy!

Mrs. Tandy began to cry, she was so happy to hear him talk.

Then Sammy said, "Why are you slopping water on my face, Kathy? Hey, cut it out!"

He started to sit up.

Dave said, "Stay down for a minute, Sammy. You were hurt. You fell and bumped your head. The man up there gave us bandages and water."

Sammy said, "So he IS up there!"

Bill looked up at the dark hole above them.

He said, "Whoever you are, thanks! I think my brother's going to be OK.

"The bleeding's pretty much stopped. Why don't you come down now?"

The man shouted, "Oh, no! No, I can't come down!"

Sammy got to his feet slowly.

He said, "Then we will come up!

We are looking for a lost dog that belongs to the Strongs. And we know she's in this house!"

The little man gave a little moan. He said, "No, no, you don't understand. The dog is mine! And you can't come up! No one must see me!"

The man was crying. He said, "You've spoiled my life. Thirty years of hiding ... all for nothing!

85

"But I can't really blame you. You didn't know what you were doing."

Sammy said, "HEY! We didn't mean to spoil your life. And we won't take your dog.

"Don't cry! And anyway, it looks like you spoiled your life yourself, by sneaking in and living here."

The man said, "But I didn't sneak in."

Dave said, "Then how did you get in?"

The man said, "I didn't have to get in! I was born here! I am the son of Ernie and Emma Bell. I'm Gordon Bell!"

Sammy said, "Hey, then it was YOU who wrote your name in the tunnel when you were a kid!"

Mrs. Tandy said, "But how can you be the Bells' child? I've lived in Bluff Lake for many, many years. I never heard the Bells had a son."

The man said, "That doesn't surprise ME. Nobody knew about me except for the three people my parents trusted.

"My parents kept me hidden until the day they died, so people wouldn't make fun of me."

Sammy said, "Why? What's so wrong with you?"

Kathy poked him in the side. She whispered, "Sammy, that's rude!"

Sammy said in a loud voice, "What's rude about asking that? I saw you once, Mr. Bell. You didn't look so awful to me!"

The man said, "That's because you were far away.

"Now go away, and leave me alone. But promise me you won't tell anyone about me for a few hours.

"I know I can't stop you from telling someone sooner or later, but will you give me a few hours to think of what to do?"

Kathy said, "Of course we will go away. And we won't tell anyone about you if you don't want us to, ever."

Mrs. Tandy said, "It's true. We won't. But I do have a question. If you never went to school, how is it that you know how to write?

"And what about those books in the library? How did you learn to read?"

The man said, "My parents taught me. They tried to make a good life for me here."

Dave said, "The Strongs must be two of the three people who know about you."

Kathy said, "And that's why your dog has their name on her tag. To keep your secret."

The voice cried, "Yes, yes, you're right!

And they're the ones who told me who you were!

"But now, please go away. I only talked to you because one of you was hurt. Now I wish you'd just leave me alone."

Sammy said, "Wait! This whole thing is a big bunch of hogwash! Why do you think you can't let anyone see you, or even talk to you!

"Your folks believed a whole bunch of hogwash, and now YOU do! Hogwash! Just hogwash!"

Bill said, "Cut it out, Sammy!"

Sammy went right on. "Of COURSE you can talk to us! You HAVE been talking to us for ten minutes already."

Kathy said, "Sammy! Come on."

But Sammy kept going.

He said, "Why should a guy sit alone in an attic for another thirty years ... just because he's done it for thirty stupid years already?"

He called up into the trap-door hole.

He said, "Mr. Bell, come down here and talk to us. We won't make fun of you, I promise! Get down here ... now!"

All was quiet.

For half a minute no one spoke.

A full minute passed.

There was no sound for a full two minutes.

Sammy began to think he had shocked the little man to death.

He called up, "Are you OK? I didn't mean to hurt your feelings."

At last the voice from the attic spoke. "What would you do ... if I were too awful for you to look at?"

Sammy said, "You're not! I told you I saw you already!"

There was another long silence.

Then the voice said, "Move the steps away. I'm coming down."

Chapter 11:
The Little Man

The Woodlanders moved the steps in a hurry.

A ladder came sliding down.

They all looked up.

First they saw the backs of the man's small shoes coming down the ladder.

Then his two child-sized legs.

Then his man-sized back.

He reached the bottom of the ladder.

He said in a quiet voice, "Now look at me if you can stand it."

Gordon Bell was about as tall as a first grader.

His head was large for his body.

His hair was black, with a little gray on the sides above his ears.

His eyes were sad.

Sammy, of course, was the first to say something.

He said, "Well, you are small, all right. Big deal. Is that why your mom and dad hid you for all those years? Just for that? Wow."

The little man looked around at the Woodlanders.

He said nothing, but he seemed to be asking them a question with his eyes.

Mrs. Tandy stepped up to him with her hand out.

She said, "I'm so glad to meet you. May we call you Gordon?   I'm Becky Tandy."

Shyly he nodded.   He shook her hand with his left hand.   He kept his right hand in his pocket.

Big-mouthed Sammy asked, "Why are you hiding your right hand?"

Inch by inch Gordon moved his hand from his pocket and held it out for them to see.

It had a thumb and only one finger.

Sammy said, "Well, it's lucky you have that one good finger! So you can still do everything.

"What if you were hurt as bad as Dave was in his accident, and you couldn't walk?"

Gordon took a close look at Dave in his wheelchair. He walked around him slowly.

He said softly, "You have it a hundred times worse than me, don't you? And you still do almost everything you want, don't you?"

Dave said, "Sure, as much as I can do. My family here helps me out a lot.

And my other friends."

Gordon said, "All these years I've been hiding and feeling sorry for myself.

"Do you think this whole time I should have been with other people? Were my folks all wrong?"

Sammy whispered to Bill, "Wrong! They were crazy as bedbugs, if you ask me."

Bill jabbed him in the ribs.

Kathy said, "It sounds like they just loved you so much, they tried to keep you from being hurt."

Mrs. Tandy said, "But they should have let you meet at least a few people. Then you'd see that EVERYONE has problems!"

Gordon said, "But what if other people aren't as nice as you?

"If they know I live here, they may come and make fun of me. And I couldn't stand that."

Dave said, "Well, let's keep your secret until you get used to US. Then you could meet more people, one at a time."

Sammy said, "Sure! We can come and visit. You can show us your place upstairs."

Kathy said, "And we could read in your library!"

Mrs. Tandy said, "And I'd make you some jelly. After all, I've been stealing plums from you for years."

Gordon just stood quietly for a long while.

Then he said, "You dear people, I can't believe I'm lucky enough to have new friends after so many years alone."

He pointed at each of them. He said, "Kathy, Becky, Sammy, Bill, and Dave. Am I right?"

Sammy said, "That's right!"

He looked into each of their faces.

Then he broke into a grin.

Suddenly he jumped up, almost to the ceiling.

He clapped his hands going up and coming down.

He shouted, "Hooray!" as he did handsprings down the hall.

Kathy gasped, "Wow! Gordon could be in the Olympics!"

He did cartwheels all the way back.

Then he stood still in front of them again.

He said with a serious look, "I certainly thank you for finding me."

Mrs. Tandy said, "Well, you're welcome!"

Sammy said, "Do you think I could learn to do some of that? Maybe after my head heals up, that is ..."

Gordon smiled. "Of course! Why not? I'll teach you. I taught myself.

"But now, follow me to the best room in the house! Dave, how will you get upstairs?"

Dave said, "If there are real stairs somewhere it's no problem. Bill and Sammy can carry me up."

He looked at Sammy's head. "Well, Bill and Mrs. Tandy can carry me up."

Gordon said, "Then follow me to the bedroom you were in before. You know, when I made the chain noise in the hall.

"I did that because you'd almost found my stairs. I heard you through the

100

listening hole."

Kathy said, "Listening hole! Do you mean you heard us talking in the bedroom?"

Gordon nodded. "Oh, yes. I put a hole in the ceiling above every room."

He walked into the bedroom, jumped up to the ceiling light, and swung on it.

A door opened in the wall behind the head of the bed.

Behind it was a stairway!

Sammy shouted, "Wow! That's great! A secret stairway!"

Gordon said, "It goes upstairs, and down into the old kitchen, and outside.

"I usually just jump into the door from the head of the bed.

"But the bed can be rolled away, and your wheelchair can fit right in there, Dave.

"I used these stairs to get into the old kitchen when you were searching my house.

"I was in a cabinet watching you when you looked around in there."

Sammy bragged, "If I had known that, I'd have grabbed you."

Bill said, "Then we'd have grabbed YOU, Sammy, to catch you when you FAINTED!"

Mrs. Tandy and Bill moved the bed and took Dave up the steps.

At the top, Gordon said, "Come in! This has been my room for thirty years. Make yourselves at home."

They stepped into a huge room, as big as a school lunchroom.

The ceiling was high, like a barn ceiling, with wooden beams across it.

A bed and dresser stood against one wall.

And the entire place was full of wonderful things ... on shelves, on the floor, and on low wooden tables.

Mrs. Tandy cried, "My stars! What's that huge net hanging from the ceiling for?"

Gordon said, "I'll show you!" He grabbed the net, and climbed it to the top.

Then he took hold of a brass pole and

slid to the floor like a fire fighter.

Bill followed after him.

Gordon also had a balance beam, swinging rings, boxing gloves, and a mat.

Bill jumped down. He said, "Is that a pool table down at that end?"

Dave wheeled down the room and shouted, "Is this a hot tub? Wow!"

Kathy said, "Hey! These books are all about medicine ... it's like a doctor's library!"

Gordon said, "I've been studying for years with Dr. Strong. He has no children of his own, and he thinks I should be a doctor. But of course I can't."

Sammy asked, "Why not?"

Gordon said, "I ... I can't go to college."

"Why not?" Sammy asked again.

As they talked, everybody was busy exploring the room.

Bill began pounding a ball of clay he had found on a table.

Mrs. Tandy opened and closed kitchen cupboards.

Kathy played "Chopsticks" on the piano.

Dave was pulling himself up the net using only his arms. He was about eight feet up in the air, yelling like Tarzan!

Princess was running around, barking at all the noise.

All of a sudden a loud voice boomed from across the room, "What in the world is going on here?"

A big, frowning police officer stood in the doorway.

Chapter 12:
A Fat Ghost

Everyone jumped with surprise.

In the doorway was Police Chief John Hemster.

In back of him stood a man and a woman.

Sammy said, "Chief Hemster! What are you doing here?"

Bill said, "Dr. Strong!"

Gordon said, "Mrs. Strong!" and jogged over to greet them.

Mrs. Tandy said, "Well, hello, Ann! Hi, Albert! Hi, John!"

Chief Hemster said, "Hi, Becky! I can't believe I'm seeing right!"

Mrs. Strong said, "Are you all right, Gordon dear?"

Gordon nodded and smiled. "More than all right! You won't believe what's happened here today!"

Mrs. Strong said, "Bring me a chair. I think I need to sit down for THIS."

He ran to get a chair. He patted her hand and said, "I didn't expect you today. You always phone first."

Dr. Strong answered, "Ann told me the Woodland family called about Princess,

Gordon. I was afraid they might come and find you here."

Gordon said, "Well, it's lucky they DID find me."

Dr. Strong said, "Gordon, I'm in shock! We three spent twenty-five years trying to get your parents to let you see people.

"And then we spent five years working on YOU, begging you and getting no-where.

"We couldn't get you to meet even ONE other person.

"And now we find you in the middle of the Woodland family! How in the world did this happen!"

Then Dr. Strong turned to Sammy. "Do I see a bandage on your head, young man? Come here and let me look at that while I hear the story."

Gordon began to tell them everything that had happened.

The Woodlanders had to tell about their walk to the Bell House the day before ... the phone call ... finding Princess ... and Sammy falling into the tree stump.

Kathy said, "When we walked up the first time, only a chipmunk and a couple of squirrels were here.

"We didn't know anyone else would be living here!"

Gordon smiled. "Oh, did my chipmunk try to get some food from you? His name is Grub. I feed him every day."

Dave said, "So THAT'S why he was so friendly!"

Then he said, "So, Chief Hemster, YOU were the other person Gordon knew all these years.

"You know everything that goes on in town, don't you?"

Mrs. Tandy said, "John Hemster, you smart old thing!

"You knew this secret all the years we've been friends, and never said one word about it.

"What else are you hiding in that handsome head of yours?"

Chief Hemster blushed.

He said, "Becky, you always know just what to say!

"Maybe you'll know what to say to Gordon here ... to get him to go to college and then medical school.

"Albert here says Gordon knows enough to pass some tests already. But that's just a start."

Sammy broke in. "Aw, Mrs. Tandy won't have to talk to Gordon about that. He won't hide anymore. He likes us.

"He's going to spend time with us, and THEN meet the rest of the world.

"THEN he will go to college and medical school."

Gordon said, "Well, Dr. Strong, I guess Sammy has my life in good shape. Maybe in a year or so I WILL apply to some colleges."

Sammy said, "A YEAR! I want you to start FAST. A year is no good!"

Bill added, "Sammy's right. Why can't you apply right now? Then you could start in a few months."

Dave said, "Sure! Then if you don't feel ready you can always change your mind."

Gordon laughed. "Well, looks like I'm going to have to apply now! All right! I give up!"

Mrs. Strong said, "Gordon, my dear. Since you think you might be able to meet other people soon, do you think you could visit our home?

"For so many years I hoped you'd come to live with us, as our son."

Sammy said, "Sure he will. And I'll visit, too. I'll help make sure nobody sees him ... if he doesn't want them to.

"On the way we can both hide under a sheet in the back seat of your car!

"Then we can walk into your house under the sheet, and the neighbors will all get screaming scared.

"They'll call Chief Hemster to report a FAT GHOST with four legs. And then he will tell them they must be seeing things. And ..."

Gordon said, "Well, if it's going to be THAT hard to hide, I guess I can ride out in the open in your car, Mrs. Strong!"

Sammy shouted, "Hooray! Let's go!"

And soon they were all making their way down the secret steps together.

Chapter 13:
The Holiday House

On a cold, dark Thanksgiving afternoon
two months later, two cars drove up to
the old Bell House.

The Woodlanders got out of one car.

Chief Hemster, the Strongs, and Gordon Bell got out of the other.

The dark old house wasn't dark anymore. The boards were off all the windows, and bright light was shining out.

The Woodlanders and their friends were carrying all sorts of big boxes and baskets into the house.

Inside were painters, cleaning up. The day before, they had finished painting all the walls white.

Mrs. Tandy said, "My, this is a lovely place now!"

Dave said, "With the paint job finished and the elevator in, the house is almost ready."

Chief Hemster said, "Come on, Becky. Let's head up with all this stuff."

They stepped into the elevator with the baskets of food. In the third-floor kitchen, they got all the food ready.

Then they covered a table with a red-and-white cloth, and put a big bowl of fruit in the middle.

Soon Mrs. Strong came up to join them. She said, "Oh, it looks perfect!"

Mrs. Tandy said, "Turning this old house into a holiday house for disabled children is a fine idea. I'm so glad you and Gordon decided to fix it up!"

Mrs. Strong said, "Yes, and I can't tell you how glad I am to have Gordon living with us now.

"This house will never again hide an un-happy child.

"You should hear Gordon talk about it … from now on this place will help children get along in the world.

"In fact, eight Boy Scouts who can't walk well are coming tomorrow."

Chief Hemster said, "Tomorrow the caretakers arrive, too, don't they?"

Mrs. Strong said, "Yes, and they're a fine pair. They'll clean the house and cook whenever children and scout leaders are here."

Chief Hemster said, "The food's all ready. Should I call everyone?"

But he didn't need to call them.

In they trooped for Thanksgiving dinner.

They all sat down and looked at the feast.

Dr. Strong smiled at everybody.

He said, "I have so much to be thankful for this year! Mostly, I'm thankful to have Gordon living with us in our home."

Mrs. Strong said, "And I want to thank the Woodlanders for their good hearts ... and good detective work."

Chief Hemster said, "I'm thankful for all these wonderful people." He looked hard at Becky Tandy.

Gordon said, "I'm thankful for a new life!"

Mrs. Tandy said, "I'm thankful for my family and all my friends. Don't worry, I won't take time to name them all!"

Dave said, "I'm thankful for new friends and old." His eyes rested on Kathy.

She blushed, and couldn't say anything at all!

Sammy said, "I'm glad to have Kathy and Dave and Mrs. Tandy and all of you. And I'm mostly glad ..." He stopped, and then blurted out, "... to have my weird brother Bill."

Bill said, "And I'm thankful to have you, Sammy! Boy, I MUST be weird!

"But enough talk, already! Let's have Thanksgiving dinner!"